The story so far . . .

On January 6, 2050, the Starseeker space station launches into orbit around the sun. Among its crew are three young friends: Noah, a back-up pilot; Sera, a rock specialist; and JiJi, an assistant in the station's animal lab. Starseeker's mission? To protect Earth from dangerous asteroids and comets.

When the station comes upon an unknown asteroid field, Noah and Sera are sent to explore strange signals coming from one of the asteroids. But as they approach their mysterious target in Noah's ARC 017 spaceship, frightening news comes from the station: a collision with asteroid fragments has caused JiJi's animal lab to separate from Starseeker!

Noah and Sera know they are the closest ship to JiJi. Fearing that his friend will be lost in space, just as his parents were three years earlier, Noah disobeys a direct order to return to Starseeker. Can he and Sera rescue JiJi before she is lost forever?

Jon W.

To our grandaughters
Lucy and Isabella,
space pioneers of the future.
—E.R. & D.B.

Library of Congress Cataloging-in-Publication Data available

12 11 10 9 8 7 6 5 4 3 2 1   00 01 02 03 04 05 06

Printed in the U.S.A.

First printing, Febrary 2000

2050
VOYAGE OF THE STARSEEKER ™

BOOK 2
RESCUE IN SPACE

ELAINE RAPHAEL & DON BOLOGNESE

SCHOLASTIC INC.

New York   Toronto   London   Auckland   Sydney
Mexico City   New Delhi   Hong Kong

1 LOST IN SPACE

time • 36 hours, 27 minutes into Noah's mission
place • JiJi's Module

"Hurry, Noah!" cried Sera. "Every second takes JiJi farther from Starseeker."

"And closer to the sun," answered Noah, as he sent more power to the main rockets. "Our problem is the fuel supply. We have enough to catch JiJi, but after that . . ."

Sera looked out of the cockpit window.

"There's the module," she said. "I hope JiJi's all right. Can we speak to her, Noah? Can she hear us?"

Noah shook his head. "Her communications were probably damaged in the collision—but we'll know soon. We're closing fast."

The module was closer. Noah and Sera could see where it had torn away from the space station.

"Get ready for a space walk," said Noah. "After I lock onto the module, we'll check its hatches. I'm afraid they were sealed in the accident."

The ARC glided closer to the module. The spaceship's magnetic claws locked on to the metallic hull.

"Got it!" yelled Noah. "Sera, it's time to visit JiJi."

"Wow, I've never felt so small," Sera's voice sounded in Noah's headset. "I'm glad we're tethered to the ship."

Their suit thrusters moved them to the module's window. As they looked in, a face appeared.

"It's Ping!" shouted Sera, seeing JiJi's pet monkey. "And there's JiJi, behind the emergency safety net."

"She looks okay, but she's trapped under a pile of cages," Noah said as he floated to a hatch. He looked at it closely. "I thought so. Its outer door is sealed. It can only be unsealed from inside."

Noah glided back to the window. "See that ring halfway up the inside wall? That's the emergency release. If someone pulls it, the hatch cover will blow—and I can connect the ARC to the module."

"Great, Noah, but who's going to pull the ring?" asked Sera. "JiJi's trapped in there and we're out here."

"You're forgetting someone," Noah said with a smile.

"Ping!" Sera shouted. "Just like he did on the moon when he grabbed those rings for JiJi." Sera stopped. "But how are we going to tell him what to do?"

"We're not—JiJi is. Watch." Noah took out a small wrench and began tapping on the module's hull.

TAP TAP . . . TAP . . . TAP TAP TAP.

Sera laughed and patted Noah on his helmet. "You're a genius, Noah. You're using Morse code."

"That's why we all had to learn it before going into space." Noah kept tapping.

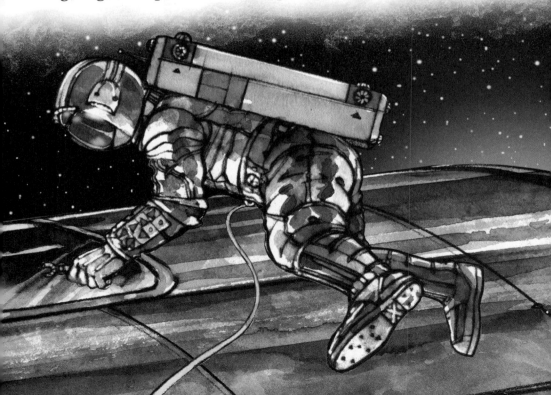

Noah and Sera watched as JiJi pointed
to the ring and made pulling motions with
her hand.

"Look," said Noah. "I think Ping's got
the idea."

JiJi's pet floated to the ring. He reached
for it.

Noah pulled Sera down alongside the hull.
"It's safer to be far from the hatch when the
bolts blow."

The bolts flew into the blackness. Noah slid down to the module's bottom hatch. Sera followed and helped him remove the outer door.

A few minutes later, they were back inside the ARC. Noah steered the ship into position under the module and locked the two hatches together.

"Okay, Sera," Noah said, as he opened the ARC's inner door. "Let's visit our new neighbor."

Noah and Sera crawled into the module's lower storage space. In the dim light they saw the emergency supplies that every module carried.

"Look, there's one of those neat space rafts," said Noah. "And I know just where we're going to use it."

Just as Sera was about to ask where, Noah climbed into the lab. Ping quickly landed on his shoulders.

"Hey, Ping, you really missed me," Noah laughed.

The other animals were howling and screaming. JiJi was crying and laughing at the same time.

Sera called, "Noah, help me free JiJi."

Minutes later, JiJi was hugging her two friends.

"Is my mom all right?" she asked. "Is Starseeker okay?"

"Don't worry, JiJi, your mom's fine. Starseeker is in good shape." Noah hugged her again. "Your lab was the only casualty."

"But that's history," Sera added. "Now we have to get back to Starseeker. Right, Noah?"

"Right!" agreed Noah. "But first we have to get the lab back in shape and feed the animals. Then we'll put Ping in charge here, go down to the ARC —"

"Then go home to Starseeker," JiJi added.

"Yes," Noah said. "Well . . . almost."

"*Almost?*" JiJi and Sera spoke at the same time.

"What does that mean?" JiJi asked.

2 THE ASTEROID

time • 40 hours, 3 minutes into Noah's mission
place • ARC's cockpit

Noah sat at the controls. The ship changed course and its speed increased. Noah pointed to the star map screen. "There's your answer, JiJi."

"What's that?" JiJi's finger was on a red dot.

"It's the asteroid," said Sera. "The weird one we were sent to probe before going after you."

"We've enough fuel to reach the asteroid but not Starseeker," said Noah.

"Oh, I get it," said JiJi. "The asteroid is halfway to Starseeker. We'll be 'almost' home."

"And this homing device will lead any Starseeker patrol ships in the area right to us," said Noah. He loaded a small cylinder into a launch tube. The ship shook as the homing device shot into space.

"We haven't eaten or slept for a while," Noah said, as he checked all the autopilot controls.

"You're right," Sera agreed. She picked some food packets out of their emergency supply.

"Here, JiJi," Sera began, then stopped. "Noah, look."

Noah turned. JiJi was sound asleep.

A few hours later, loud beeping sounds from the radar woke Sera. Their target was in sight.

"Noah, JiJi, wake up! The asteroid is straight ahead." Sera looked out the cockpit window. "Wow, that rock is much bigger than it looks on radar."

Noah steered toward a large, flat ledge on one side of the asteroid. "Here's the plan, guys. We land, secure the ARC, check on Ping and his friends, and—"

"Break out the space raft," Sera cut in, "and go exploring."

Noah laughed, " You guessed it."

"I hope you're not leaving me here," JiJi said.

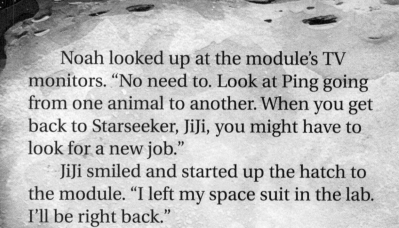

Noah looked up at the module's TV monitors. "No need to. Look at Ping going from one animal to another. When you get back to Starseeker, JiJi, you might have to look for a new job."

JiJi smiled and started up the hatch to the module. "I left my space suit in the lab. I'll be right back."

As soon as JiJi left, Sera turned to Noah. "Look at the scanner. Remember the strange signals the asteroid was sending the first time we were here?"

"I remember," said Noah. "You called them weird."

"Well," Sera whispered, "now they're beyond weird."

After boarding the raft, Noah slowly steered it along the side of the asteroid. Sera kept an eye on her scanner. Behind them, JiJi controlled the craft's solar panels.

"Noah," JiJi spoke into her intercom, "am I getting maximum power for the thrusters?"

"You're doing great, JiJi."

"Noah," Sera called out. "There—to the right."

JiJi and Noah looked in that direction. Something gleamed in the slanting sunlight.

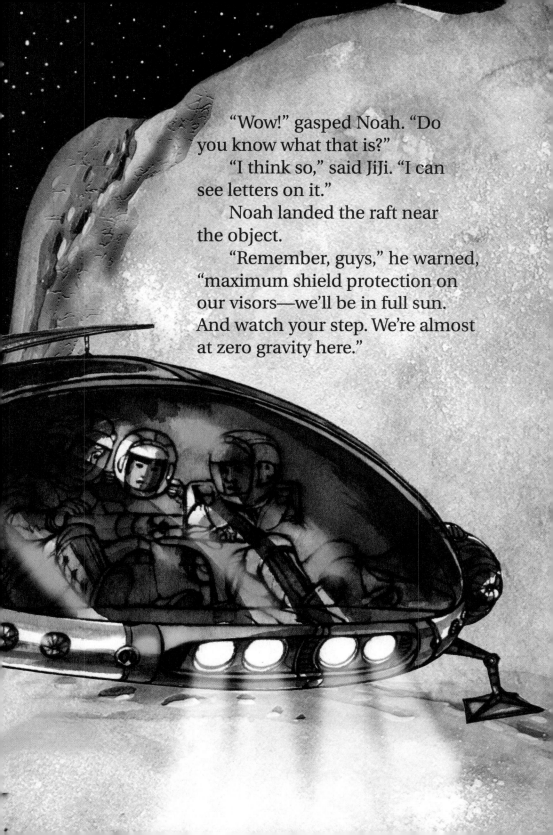

"Wow!" gasped Noah. "Do you know what that is?"

"I think so," said JiJi. "I can see letters on it."

Noah landed the raft near the object.

"Remember, guys," he warned, "maximum shield protection on our visors—we'll be in full sun. And watch your step. We're almost at zero gravity here."

Noah was right; there was just enough gravity to keep them from floating away. They bent over the metal fragment to get a closer look.

"There's a U, an N," JiJi said, pointing, "part of an I. United—United Space Agency! It's part of an Agency spaceship." JiJi sounded very excited.

"If that's true," said Noah, "then this piece can't be more than five

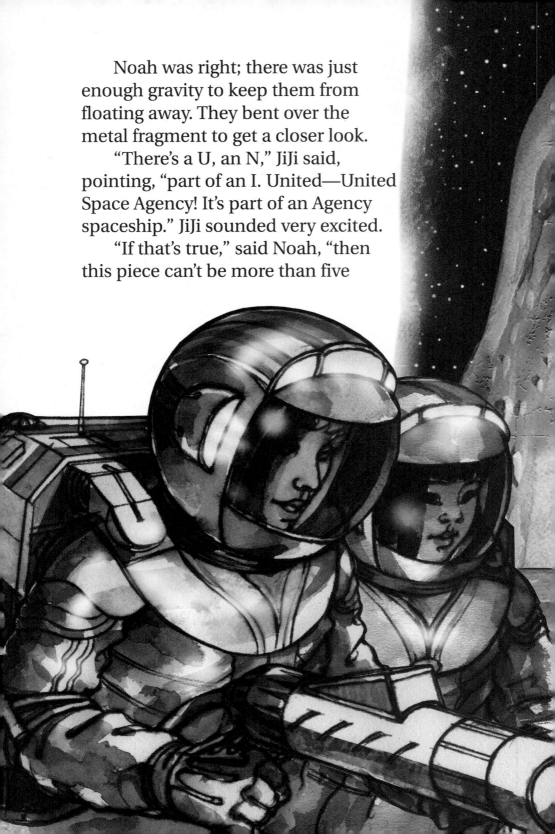

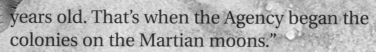

years old. That's when the Agency began the colonies on the Martian moons."

Noah picked up the piece of metal. All three friends had the same thought. *Was this part of Noah's parents' ship? Did it mean his parents were alive?*

Noah was about to speak when he felt the ground shake. JiJi and Sera felt it, too. Sera's scanner was going crazy!

Sera swung the scanner, then stopped. "The vibrations are stronger there." She led the way to a large hole. It went into the asteroid at a steep angle.

"Another surprise," said Sera. "This hole was drilled."

"Who could have done it?" asked JiJi.

"Maybe researchers or miners," Noah said. "If we find the source of the vibrations, we might find some answers." Noah turned to JiJi. "Wait for us here. We'll be back soon."

Sera and Noah started down the hole.

"No!" JiJi's helmet shook from side to side. "I'm going with you."

"It's too dangerous," Noah explained.

Sera tapped Noah and pointed to her intercom. Noah nodded and changed the channel.

"Noah, I know that this tunnel could be dangerous, but the truth is, this whole plan is risky. What if the homing device fails and no one comes for us? JiJi doesn't want to face that by herself."

Noah nodded. "You're right, Sera. It is better if we stay together." He switched to the other channel. "Okay, JiJi, follow us. But stay back a bit and keep your flashlight on full power."

3 THE TUNNEL

time • 48 hours, 23 minutes into Noah's mission
place • Tunnel on the mystery asteroid

Sera led the way into the tunnel. The vibrations got stronger. Sera stopped to examine the walls.

"I'm sure about one thing," she said. "Space miners have been here."

"But only known asteroids can be mined," Noah said. "This one wasn't reported to Starseeker. Why?"

"Greed," answered Sera. "Whoever found this one didn't want to share it. It's very rich in rare metals."

"Sera, Noah!" JiJi called out. "Do you feel that?" Her hand was on the wall. "The whole wall is shaking."

Sera quickly aimed her scanner in that direction.

"JiJi! Get back! Fast!" she yelled.

A shower of rock burst into the tunnel. JiJi screamed. The tunnel filled with dust.

"JiJi, Sera, are you all right?" Noah felt someone push by him. It was Sera. She crawled over the rocks and aimed her flashlight at a hole in the wall.

The vibrations stopped. The dust settled. With his flashlight, Noah could see a giant drill. It had broken through the wall, cutting them off from JiJi—and the surface.

He called to JiJi over the intercom.

"I'm okay," her voice was shaky. "Is Sera all right?"

"Yes," Sera answered, "but we're trapped."

Noah broke in. "Sera, why did the drill stop?"

"See the panel that's lit up? That's a light sensor. For safety reasons these drills stop when they sense light. As long as I keep my flashlight on it, the drill won't go forward—I hope."

"Can you fit through the space that's left?" JiJi asked.

"We can't risk it," Noah answered. "The drill could tear our suits."

"Do you have a plan?" JiJi asked.

"I think I can make the drill back up," Sera said calmly. "And you, JiJi, are going to do it. Get a wrench from your tool pack."

"Got it," JiJi said, eager to help.

"Crawl into the hole and look for the manual control panel on the drill face," said Sera. "Remove the cover."

Noah and Sera waited while JiJi carefully followed Sera's instructions. They didn't breathe.

"It's open!" JiJi shouted. "What's next?"

At that moment, the center drill started to turn.

"What's happening?" JiJi cried.

Sera thought fast. "Nothing—that's normal. Find the reverse button on the control panel. Push it and hold it in for a second. Then get out of the hole—quickly!"

JiJi followed Sera's orders. The big disk began to turn. Slowly, the drill backed up into the hole it had made in the tunnel wall.

"C'mon, Noah. Let's get out of here."

"What's wrong, Sera?"

Sera switched channels so JiJi couldn't hear.

"Listen, Noah, when that screw bit began turning, I told JiJi it was normal. It's not. Someone started that drill. Any second now they'll notice it's going in the wrong direction—so move!"

They were almost past the rock pile when Noah tapped Sera.

"The vibrations—they've changed."

They both turned to look just as the screw bit came crashing back. They scrambled out of its way. The drill dug into the opposite wall and kept going.

4 SPACE MINERS

time • 50 hours, 43 minutes into Noah's mission
place • Surface of the mysterious asteroid

Back on the surface, the three friends stopped to put the metal fragment in the raft.

"Everybody in position? We're lifting off." Noah fired the thrusters. The raft climbed slowly.

"JiJi, you did a great job down there," Noah smiled.

"I have to admit," said JiJi, "I was really scared."

"We were *all* scared," Sera added.

"I'm confused, Sera," said JiJi. "I know I pushed the reverse button. Why did the drill go forward again?"

"Attention, crew," Noah broke in. "We're almost at the top of the asteroid. And I have a feeling that all our questions are about to be answered."

Just as Noah finished speaking, the space raft rose above the rim of the asteroid.

"What is *that?*" JiJi shouted.

"A giant ore collector! This is the first one
I've seen in action." Sera was impressed.

"And that's an ore carrier," Sera went on, pointing
to a large, bulky ship. "It's probably loading up for a
trip to the factories on the Martian moon Phobos."

"JiJi, there's your answer to who started the
drill." Noah pointed to the scene below them.
"Space miners. They can help us contact Starseeker."

Sera shook her head. "Something's not right. Their sensors must have told them we're here. Why haven't they come for us?"

JiJi tapped her friend on the shoulder. "They just did," she said.

Two astronauts hovered in space behind the raft.

"Follow us," an unfriendly voice ordered.

Noah quickly changed intercom channels. JiJi and Sera followed his lead.

"Any thoughts about what's going to happen?" Noah asked, as he steered the space craft to a nearby landing area.

"They don't look very happy to see us, do they?" Sera answered.

"We're members of Starseeker," JiJi said firmly. "They have to help us."

"They should," Noah said, "but they may not want Starseeker patrols checking on them."

"Right," added Sera, "especially if they're breaking Rule 1."

"What's that?" asked JiJi.

"No explosives," answered Sera. "Because when an asteroid explodes, nobody knows where all of the fragments go. Anyplace, including Earth, could become a target."

"My lab was hit by rocks that came from nowhere," said JiJi.

The space raft landed. The men motioned the three Starseeker crew members to follow them.

They were led to an air lock built into a cavern. As they went in alone, the air lock filled with air. The oxygen lights on their arm panels flashed.

"Okay to lift your visors," Noah said, as the air lock's inner door opened into another cavern.

Computer screens and TV monitors covered one wall. On another wall, a three-dimensional holograph of the solar system stretched from floor to ceiling. A man stood watching it. His back was to them.

Noah could tell he was studying Starseeker's orbit. Finally, the man spoke.

"Three months, maybe four. Then I would have been done with this rock. But you had to blunder into it, didn't you, Noah?" He turned to face them.

Noah felt a chill run up his back.

Sera's right, he thought. *They've been tracking us.* As Noah started to answer, JiJi stepped forward.

"Sir, my name is JiJi, and I'm in charge of the animals in the module. If they don't return to Starseeker soon, they'll die." She took a deep breath and pointed to the holograph. "There's Starseeker. You must contact them and tell them where we are!"

The man's laughter bounced off the cavern's walls. It felt like sharp rocks were hitting their helmets.

"I MUST?" he shouted, and laughed again.

He stepped toward JiJi. Noah and Sera jumped to her side. The man stopped. His face was like a stone when he spoke.

"You will leave this asteroid when I'm done with it."

He pressed a button at his waist. When his men came in, he motioned for the three to be taken away. The guards pushed them toward the air lock.

Noah spun around and faced their boss.

"Are you going to return us to Starseeker? Or are we your prisoners?"

The air lock door slammed shut.

Noah stood next to his two friends, trying to control his anger. He saw Sera switching her channels. She held up three fingers, then two. Noah tuned to channel 32.

"Are those our orders?" he overheard a guard ask.

"Yes," said the other one. "We put the kids on our ore carrier. Then turn their ships into space junk."

"Understood," said the first guard. "Just like the last time. The boss never leaves any evidence."

Noah felt sick. *This is all my fault,* he thought. *I never should have gone after JiJi on my own.*

JiJi turned to look at her friends. *I have to be strong,* she thought. She tried to remember what her grandfather told her about being brave. She looked up. A very bright star, just above the asteroid, caught her eye. It seemed to grow larger and brighter. *Is that possible?* she asked herself.

"Noah, Sera, look!" JiJi pointed to the star.

The guards saw it, too.

5 RESCUE

time • 50 hours, 57 minutes into Noah's mission
place • Miner's camp on the asteroid

"That's not a star," Noah said, as he switched his visor to telescopic mode.

The guards did, too. What they saw made them run. One to the cavern; the other to the ore collector.

"What is it?" Sera's visor wasn't like Noah's.

JiJi began waving and pointing to her helmet.

"Switch channels, Noah!" Sera shouted.

"ARC 017, this is Captain Ryan on LRC 01, come in ARC 017. Captain Ryan calling ARC 017, come in."

"I knew it!" Noah yelled. "I knew it was a ship, but I couldn't be sure it was ours."

"Call! Tell them we're here," Sera said.

"Please, Noah, tell them to hurry!" JiJi pleaded.

"Our suit transmitters are too weak, but this is just as good." Noah pulled a flare launcher out of his emergency kit. He fired it. Sera and JiJi watched as it exploded high above the asteroid.

"The cruiser knows we're here now," Noah said.

"And not a minute too soon," Sera answered. "Look who's back."

"You are very lucky, Cadet Noah, and smart," said the mining boss. "I'm sure your parents will be very proud of you."

The guards smiled at their boss' words. Sera grabbed Noah's arm.

"You can't do anything to us," she said. "That flare told Starseeker we're here—and alive."

"Breaking mining rules is one thing." Noah's voice was angry. "But kidnapping us . . ."

"I don't have time for your lectures, young man." The boss waved to his men. As they headed for the space raft, he turned to face Noah.

"I like your raft, Noah. I have a couple of engineers who can turn it into a perfect little mining craft."

"When the Captain's ship gets here, your mining days will be over," Noah shot back.

"Your Captain will be too busy to think about me." The space mining boss snapped the raft's canopy shut and took off.

The three friends watched the raft glide to the ore carrier. Sera turned to Noah.

"Too busy. What does that mean, Noah?"

"It means that I'd better check the control room. The cruiser will be here soon. I'll be back."

It took only two leaps for Noah to get to the cavern.

Noah looked at the computer screens. One, with a 3-D model of the asteroid, was flashing. A panel displayed the minutes to detonation: 30 minutes, 27 seconds. *Not much time to collect any evidence,* Noah thought.

He looked around the control room. All he saw was a small box. He took it, and rushed to the landing area, just as the cruiser arrived. A crew member hurried them on board.

"Noah," Sera asked, "why are they rushing us?"

Checking the time, Noah said, "They must know
what I just found out—the whole asteroid is ready
to blow in exactly 21 minutes, 24 seconds."

"Ping! The lab! They'll be blown up," cried JiJi, as
they went through the air lock.

"Don't worry, JiJi," Captain Ryan said. "I've taken
good care of them." She turned to Noah. "Thanks
to your homing device, we got here in time. Now
we have to get as far from this rock as possible."
She called to her co-pilot, "Full power. Now!"

6 A CLUE FOR NOAH

time • The next day
place • Starseeker's main deck

"Mom!" JiJi flew into her mother's arms.

Dr. Wu hugged her daughter tightly. She turned to JiJi's friends. "Your bravery and loyalty saved JiJi's life. I will remember that always."

"Excuse me, Dr. Wu," Captain Ryan spoke softly. "The Commander is waiting to see Noah and Sera." As they walked, the Captain spoke to Noah.

"You did well out there, Cadet. You flew with skill and used your head. But you disobeyed an order. That is not acceptable on a space station. I'm putting you on six-months probation. You've earned a second chance, Noah. Use it well."

"I'm happy to see you safely back home," the Commander greeted them. "You had a close call."

A face looked out at them from a monitor on the Commander's desk. Noah and Sera gasped.

"That's him, sir, the space miner," Sera said.

"We've heard about this miner before," the Commander said. "He finds an asteroid, keeps it a secret, mines it, then blows it up. There has never been any proof that Mr. Starrk was breaking the law, until now."

"Sir? Is that his name, Starrk?" Noah asked.

"Yes. And you, Sera, and JiJi are the witnesses we need to remove this dangerous man from space."

The Commander continued, "Sera's scans of the metal fragment prove that a ship was on that asteroid. We tested the flight recorder that was in the box you found, Noah, but it is too damaged." He pointed to the monitor. "Only a few word fragments and some number sequences."

Noah moved closer to the screen. He scrolled the numbers several times.

"Noah?" Sera asked. "Did you find something?"

"One sequence, 6–7–2036, keeps showing up, like a code or password." Noah picked up the blackened flight recorder. He stared at it for a long time. His thoughts were far away.

The Commander put his hand on Noah's shoulder.

"Does the number sequence mean anything to you?"

"Yes," answered Noah. "It's the date of my birth, sir."

**The Voyage of the Starseeker
continues . . . the mystery deepens.**